# Juliet
### nearly a
# Vet

## Bush Baby Rescue

REBECCA JOHNSON

Illustrated by Kyla May

For Mum and Dad
The kindest people I know. RJx

PUFFIN BOOKS

Published by the Penguin Group
Penguin Group (Australia)
707 Collins Street, Melbourne, Victoria 3008, Australia
(a division of Penguin Australia Group Pty Ltd)
Penguin Group (USA) Inc.
375 Hudson Street, New York, New York 10014, USA
Penguin Group (Canada)
90 Eglinton Avenue East, Suite 700, Toronto, Canada ON M4P 2Y3
(a division of Penguin Canada Books Inc.)
Penguin Books Ltd
80 Strand, London WC2R 0RL England
Penguin Ireland
25 St Stephen's Green, Dublin 2, Ireland
(a division of Penguin Books Ltd)
Penguin Books India Pvt Ltd
11 Community Centre, Panchsheel Park, New Delhi – 110 017, India
Penguin Group (NZ)
67 Apollo Drive, Rosedale, Auckland 0632, New Zealand
(a division of Penguin New Zealand Pty Ltd)
Penguin Books (South Africa) (Pty) Ltd, Rosebank Office Park, Block D,
181 Jan Smuts Avenue, Parktown North, Johannesburg, 2196, South Africa
Penguin (Beijing) Ltd
7F, Tower B, Jiaming Center, 27 East Third Ring Road North,
Chaoyang District, Beijing 100020, China

Penguin Books Ltd, Registered Offices: 80 Strand, London, WC2R 0RL, England

First published by Penguin Group (Australia), 2013

Text copyright © Rebecca Johnson, 2013
Illustrations copyright © Kyla May Productions, 2013

The moral right of the author and illustrator has been asserted.

All rights reserved. Without limiting the rights under copyright reserved above, no part of this
publication may be reproduced, stored in or introduced into a retrieval system, or transmitted, in
any form or by any means (electronic, mechanical, photocopying, recording or otherwise), without
the prior written permission of both the copyright owner and the above publisher of this book.

Cover and text design by Karen Scott © Penguin Group (Australia)
Illustrations by Kyla May Productions
Typeset in New Century Schoolbook
Colour separation by Splitting Image Colour Studio, Clayton, Victoria
Printed and bound in Australia by Griffin Press

National Library of Australia
Cataloguing-in-Publication data:

Johnson, Rebecca.
Bush Baby Rescue/Rebecca Johnson; illustrated by Kyla May.

ISBN: 978 0 14 330714 3 (pbk.)

A823.4

puffin.com.au

MIX
Paper from
responsible sources
FSC® C009448
www.fsc.org

Hi! I'm Juliet. I'm ten years old.
And I'm nearly a vet!

I bet you're wondering how someone who is only ten
could nearly be a vet. It's pretty simple really.
My mum's a vet. I watch what she does and
I help out all the time. There's really not that
much to it, you know...

# CHAPTER 1

## Vets Hate Bushfires

I can't sleep. It's *so* hot I can't even stand to have a sheet over me and the fan just seems to be pushing blankets of hot air onto me. I carefully step over Curly, my cocker spaniel who's asleep on the floor, to open my window some more. Mum and Dad and Chelsea's parents are standing silently outside on the pavement in the middle of the night. What's going on?

I go outside to talk to them. Curly wakes and follows me. It's as if he knows something is wrong. That's when I see the eerie glow on the horizon in the distance.

'What's that?' I ask.

'There's a massive bushfire on the mountain range,' says Dad, putting his arm around my shoulder.

I smell the smoke as we all stand and watch the orange line that snakes across the horizon. Suddenly I start to panic. 'Isn't that where Maisy lives?'

'No, honey,' Mum reassures me. 'Maisy lives further west, but there *are* houses up in those mountains, and a lot of bushland.' She looks really worried.

'Come on,' Dad says. 'We'd better try

and get some sleep. It's going to be a busy day tomorrow.'

'Why? What have we got on tomorrow?' I ask.

Mum takes my hand. 'Juliet, there are going to be a lot of very badly hurt animals coming out of that fire. I don't know if it's a good idea for you to be at home. Perhaps you and Chelsea could go out to Maisy's farm for the weekend?'

I can't believe what I'm hearing.

'Mum, I'm *nearly* a vet, and Chelsea, Maisy and I have all proved that we are very useful in a disaster. Don't you remember the cow in the dam? You'll need us tomorrow. We're not going anywhere!' I put my hands on my hips.

Mum looks over at Chelsea's mum who shrugs. 'We can see how bad it gets and make a decision on it tomorrow, Rachel.'

Mum nods and I try not to cheer.

We say goodnight, but there's no way I will sleep now. As soon as I'm back in my room I whip out my Vet Diary and start making a list of the things I'm going to need. Curly is glad I'm awake and positions himself perfectly for a pat.

- little blankets
- pillow slips
- tissues
- ice packs
- heat pads
- bottles
- formula

Mum taps on my door. She's seen my light on.

'Juliet, please go to sleep. You'll be tired all day tomorrow and being cranky won't help me at all.'

I hear the back door close softly and realise Mum has gone over to her surgery. She hasn't come back by the time I finally drift off to sleep.

# CHAPTER 2

## Vets Have to Work Quickly

I think it is the smell of the smoke
that wakes me. It's much stronger
than last night. Then I hear the
sound of people talking outside my
window. I look out and see a number
of cars pulled up on the street and
people carrying towel bundles and
pet carriers into Mum's surgery. It's
started already.

I throw on some clothes and a pair
of thongs and Curly and I race out the
back door. As I open the door to Mum's

surgery, I can see what she meant last night about badly hurt animals. The room is full of people talking quietly and looking in cages and boxes and taking them to different parts of the surgery. There is at least one other vet helping Mum and some vet nurses too.

I push my way through the confusion and look for Mum. A nurse tells me she's on the phone to the animal hospital at the university. It sounds like they're sending some of the really badly injured animals there.

When she gets off the phone, Mum is instantly surrounded by people asking her questions about what to do with all kinds of animals. She tries to answer each one as quickly as she can as she straps ice packs to a baby wombat's burnt feet and checks his heart rate. Vets do that to see if an animal's in shock.

'What can I do?' I ask Mum when she's finally alone for a minute.

Mum wipes her cheek with the back of her arm, leaving a streak of ash on her face. It's stinking hot in the surgery even though the air-conditioner is on full bore.

'Can you make sure every cage has a clean towel and water ready for when the animals go in? They're all very dehydrated. And can you race over to the house and get as many ice packs and ice cubes as you can and put them in the surgery freezer? Can you also ask Dad to get more of the old pet carriers out of the shed and scrub them down, please?'

I scribble it into my Vet Diary to make sure I don't forget anything.

Animal cages:
- water and towels
- ice
- pet carriers

I finish the water and towels as quickly as I can. A lot of the cages already have animals in them. I can see possums, sugar gliders, birds and lots of tiny wrapped-up bundles. The ones that are not too badly injured or burned try to hide from me; the others are too sick to care. They look so sad with their blackened and singed fur. I take a deep breath and try not to cry. I know if I do, Mum will send me away.

I see Dad over the other side of the room. He is holding a bundle with a fluffy possum tail hanging down. The other vet is checking it. Dad doesn't like animals very much. He doesn't even like holding my gorgeous guinea pigs. I feel very proud of him.

I squeeze through the crowd to get to him.

'What are you smiling at?' he says. 'And before you ask – no, we cannot keep it.'

I smile even more. 'Mum asked if you could get the rest of the pet carriers out of the shed and scrub them down? But if you get them out, I can wash them. I can see you're busy!'

Dad nods and I run out of the surgery. I see Chelsea coming out of her house. 'Quick, come over,' I call. 'We've got so much to do.'

11

Chelsea doesn't need to be asked twice. She races over and listens as I go through the list.

'I'll get the ice,' I say. 'Can you start washing the pet carriers Dad gets out of the shed? That's when he finishes *cuddling* the animals, of course!'

Chelsea pulls a face. 'Seriously?'

'Seriously,' I laugh. 'Isn't it amazing?'

As Chelsea dashes off, a woman walks up to me. She is carrying a shirt with something wrapped inside it. Curly assumes it is a present for him and wags his tail.

'Do you know if they have room to take one more?'

She opens the towel to reveal the most adorable baby koala I have ever seen. His little eyes are watering so badly from the smoke, it looks like he's crying.

I hold out my arms to take him. 'I'm Juliet. My mother's the vet. I'll take him straight in to her.'

'Thank you,' says the woman.

As soon as I take the baby koala Curly starts to whimper jealously. He is obviously confused by all the commotion. I'll have to put him inside for the day. Through the shirt I feel the little koala shaking as I head to the surgery. 'It's all right,' I whisper. 'I'm nearly a vet. I'll take care of you.'

A vet nurse takes him from me and heads to the area where the vets are assessing the injuries. All the taps are running as they gently wash the animals' burns and wipe the soot from their eyes and noses.

I race back out to get the ice and see that Dad and Chelsea are hard at it scrubbing the pet carriers.

In the kitchen I find Max, my five-year-old brother, sitting at the table. He has about ten dinosaurs in front of him and an empty plate.

'What are you doing?' I ask.

'Waiting for Mum to make the pancakes,' he says.

I fill a large container with ice cubes and ice packs. 'Mum's not cooking pancakes today. If you look outside you'll see why.'

'But it's Saturday. We always have pancakes on Saturday. I promised my dinosaurs.'

'Well, you and your dinosaurs are just going to have to hunt for your own food today,' I snap.

Max's lip starts to quiver and he grabs his biggest dinosaur and heads outside. I lock Curly inside and follow with the ice. Max runs over towards the surgery.

'Hey, Max,' calls Dad, 'don't go in there, buddy. Mum's really busy today.'

'But I want pancakes!' He's fully crying now. Chelsea and I roll our eyes.

'How about I make you some pancakes for lunch instead?' says Dad.

'Will you make enough for my dinosaurs?' whines Max.

'I'll make a *hugeasaurus* pile. How does that sound?'

I groan and head back to the surgery.

# CHAPTER
## 3

## Calling All Apprentice Vets

Things have quietened down a lot.
Mum is now sitting down and giving
something a tiny little bottle. It's a
baby possum. It is *sooooo* cute.

'Where is everyone?' I say.

'All of the worst cases have gone
on to the University Hospital and
the sanctuary. The wildlife carers
have taken as many as they can.
We've decided I'll handle the rest of
the orphans and less injured animals
here.' Mum gently wipes the milk from

the little possum's chin. It hangs onto the teat with tiny little paws. They look a bit like little pink hands with long nails. They are gorgeous.

'What happened to the baby koala?' I'm almost afraid to ask.

'He's hanging on, but his back feet are badly burned. I've given him something for the shock so I hope he'll settle down a bit and sleep. I haven't tried to feed him yet.'

'Can I feed something?'

Mum puts the tiny possum back into its soft material pouch and I follow her to another room where a cage and heat pad are waiting. The room is warm and dark, except for a dim light in the corner. The animals in here are mostly nocturnal and they are afraid of bright lights. It also needs to be very quiet. Vets need to know these sorts of things when they are treating wildlife. There are pet carriers and boxes everywhere and the cages all have bundles in them.

'I think with this many babies we will all need to help. The carers have taken a lot, but there are still so many here,' sighs Mum.

'I can feed heaps of them,' I whisper. 'I'll help you. I'll go and . . . '

'Juliet, slow down,' says Mum. 'There is more to this than you think. I'm going to need to teach you how to do it very carefully, otherwise they'll die.'

'Can Chelsea help? And Maisy? Can you train all of us at once?'

'Actually . . . ' Mum pauses to consider my offer. 'That's a really good idea. I'll never be able to feed them all on my own. We can run a class and do it all together.'

We leave the room just as the door to the surgery opens and Dad and Chelsea come in carrying the clean, dry pet carriers.

'Chelsea, guess what?' I whisper. 'Mum's going to teach us how to give the orphan babies a bottle. She needs our help!'

Chelsea claps her hand over her mouth and her eyes bulge. She is as excited as I am.

'We'll go and phone Maisy and get her mum to bring her over. Dad, you stay here and cuddle more animals. You need the practice,' I say.

Mum smiles for the first time that day.

❖

Maisy's mum says she will bring
Maisy over straightaway and offers to
stay and join our class. Chelsea's mum
arrives too to see what she can do.

'Would you be able to sew lots of
pouches, Helen?' asks Mum. 'I have
some old sheets and pillowcases that
you could cut up.'

They talk about the different sizes
and shapes we'll need and Chelsea's
mum heads off to get started.

'Now,' says Mum. 'The first, most
important thing we need to do is work
out exactly what animals we've got
here and sort them into groups. We'll
need to weigh them, measure them,
check for injuries and dehydration . . .'

'Hang on, Mum.' I start to rule up a table in my Vet Diary.

When I'm finished I show it to Mum. She is impressed. Vets need to be *very* organised.

Mum moves from cage to cage examining each animal and calling out information. She checks heart rate, breathing, colour of gums and for any signs of burns or injury. We set up different areas for each group of animals as we go.

Chelsea fills in the table and Mum passes each animal to me after she has made the assessment so that it can be placed in the right area. We decide that all the really weak, dehydrated babies will go in the cages along the wall and the others can go in the pet carriers in the corners of the room.

It takes us more than two hours to process all the animals and fill in my table. By the time we are finished we have:

- 15 animals that are going to need the greatest amount of care and feeding during the night.

- 9 animals that still need bottles but are starting to eat some solid food so they don't need feeding at night.

- 3 animals (one blue-tongue lizard and two birds) that can be released back into the wild when they are well enough and have recovered from their injuries.

| Animal | Condition | Weight | Length – not including tail | Number of feeds a day | Group |
|---|---|---|---|---|---|
| ringtail possum | Dehydrated and weak. Very fine fur. | 65g | 10 cm | 5 | A |
| ringtail possum | Quite alert and strong. | 200g | 17cm | 4 | B |
| brushtail possum | Healthy and alert. Very fine fur. | 120g | 14cm | 5 | A |
| adult blue tongue lizard | Missing part of its tail from fire. Very dull and quiet. | 510g | 52cm | Will need a variety of meat, insects, vegetables and fruit each day until burns heal. | C |
| sugar glider twins | Alert and fully furred. | 20g | 6cm | 4 | B |
| koala | Short sleek fur. Burnt feet. | 300g | 18cm | 6-7. Koalas do better if fed on demand. They need special formula etc. | A |

# CHAPTER
4

## Vets Need to Make Schedules

'This is going to be a huge job,' says Mum as she sits at her surgery desk and looks over the list.

Just then the door opens and Mrs Brown, Maisy and Max walk in. Max is carrying a dinosaur and eating a pancake. There are bits of pancake hanging out of the dinosaur's mouth.

Mrs Brown walks straight up to Mum and gives her a hug. 'I hear you've had a tough day?'

'I think my worst ever.' Mum looks

like she's going to cry. 'So many of them were so badly hurt, Marg.'

'How can we help?' she says.

'I guess if I can show you all how to feed and toilet them, we can start getting into a routine.'

'Toilet them!' Max blurts out laughing. 'Are you going to put them on the toilet?'

'Don't you have some dinosaurs that need feeding?' I snap.

'Well actually, I have something I really need your help with, Max,' Mum says. 'Come and have a look.'

She leads him over to the blue-tongue lizard that is lying under a warm lamp in a box.

Max nearly drops his pancake and looks up at Mum. 'Wow. Can I have it?'

'Well, no, you can't *have* it. We can't *keep* any of these animals because they are wild animals, not pets.' For some reason she glances in my direction as she speaks. 'But he will need taking care of for a few weeks until his burns heal. I wondered if you could help me out and look after him in your room. Dad could get that big old fish tank out of the shed for –'

Max is out the door and on his way to find Dad before Mum has even finished. We all hear him yelling, 'Dad, Mum's giving me a dinosaur. A real one!'

I snigger. Dad is going to be *so* excited. We all know how much he loves animals inside the house.

The rest of us stand around Mum's table and get ready for her to teach us how to feed the babies. Just as Mum's about to pick up the baby ringtail possum, the door opens and Chelsea's

mum walks in, carrying a washing
basket full of pouches.

'That was so quick!' cries Mum.
'How did you manage to sew all of
those in such a short time?'

'I got the boys to cut up the material
while I sewed,' she says, smiling.

I can't help but grin. Chelsea has
four very noisy big brothers who are
really into cars and football and stuff.
I can't imagine them helping with
sewing! It really is a day of surprises.

Mum puts the possum in one of
the pouches and Chelsea's mum stays
while we learn how to feed orphaned
baby mammals. I have my Vet Diary
out to take lots of notes as Mum talks.

1. Sterilise the bottle and teat by boiling them in clean tap water.
2. Mix up the formula for the day. Be very careful to stick to the exact amounts. Too watery or too thick will make them sick and can kill them.
3. Measure the exact amount needed for that feed, put it in a bottle, attach the teat and place it next to you with a cup of warm water.
4. Carefully open the pouch and try to find the baby's little bottom.

Chelsea gives Mum a strange look at this last instruction. 'Don't you feed them through their mouth?'

'Of course, Chelsea,' Mum smiles. 'But we have to make sure they have been to the toilet before we feed them, otherwise they get sick. In the wild their mothers lick their bottoms when

32

they want them to go to the toilet so that they don't dirty their pouch.'

Chelsea holds onto my arm for support. 'Please tell me you're not going to lick its bottom, Mrs Fletcher.'

Now we are all killing ourselves laughing. Chelsea has had to sit down.

'No, honey, we use a tissue moistened with warm water, like this.' Mum demonstrates on the tiny fluffy bottom that is now poking out of the pouch. I go back to my notes:

5. Use the damp tissue to wipe from the tummy to the tail in gentle sweeps.

'See, there she goes,' says Mum. 'She thinks it's her mum's tongue.'

We all lean in to see little beads of yellow urine coming from the baby possum's bottom. Mum dabs at them with the tissue. 'Oh, good girl,' she says as the little possum does a tiny poo.

'Oh!' gasps Chelsea. 'They poo too? I don't think I can do this.'

'It's okay, Chelsea,' says Maisy. 'You can make up the formula and I'll wipe their bottoms. I come from a dairy farm. I see more poo in one day than you probably will in a lifetime. A little extra won't kill me. I'm just glad I don't have to do that to a cow!'

'Thanks, Maisy,' laughs Chelsea.

Mum continues.

6. Keep the baby in the pouch as much as possible (it will feel safer that way). Wrap it up so that just its head is sticking out.

7. Place the bottle in the warm water for about 30 seconds to warm the milk. Test it on your wrist to see that it is not hot at all, just a little bit warm.

8. Place the teat on the baby's lips and let a little milk drip out. Some babies will take the teat straightaway and others will just lick at the drips for a while. You have to be very patient and go at their speed. You can't just pour it down their throats.

We all lean in to watch as the little possum licks at the milk and then takes the teat into her mouth. She closes her eyes and suckles the warm milk. Her little hand rests on Mum's finger. I can't wait to have a turn.

'If they drink all the milk do you give them more?' asks Chelsea's mum.

'Definitely not,' says Mum. 'They are only supposed to drink 10 to 20 per cent of their body weight a day. So, if a possum weighs 60 grams, it will need 6 to 12 millilitres of milk a day. If it has six feeds, each one will only be one to two millilitres. Overfeeding is just as bad for them as underfeeding. The girls and I have weighed them all and

we'll work out how much they need at
each feed.'

Chelsea's mum nods.

9. Don't over or under feed.
10. Wrap the baby up and put it back into its warm, dark home until the next feed.

Chelsea, Maisy and I agree that
it'll work best if we divide the babies
that need feeding during the day
only between us. Maisy's mum feels
confident enough to be able to take
three of the smaller but healthier
possums home with her. She's used
to getting up at night to feed lambs
and things on the farm. She also has

a large bird aviary that the two birds with singed feathers can go in until they are ready to fly again.

'I can come over to the surgery and help feed every four hours during the night,' offers Chelsea's mum. 'I had plenty of practice getting up to feed my five babies, and these ones don't even cry!'

'And they're a lot cuter than four of yours!' adds Chelsea.

# CHAPTER 5

## Vets Like to Stay Close to their Patients

'This is like feeding tiny stuffed toys, only better,' whispers Maisy as we feed our babies for the first time.

Their little bodies feel so warm in their pouches and their tiny eyes peep out at us confused. At first I am scared that I won't do it properly, but then my possum starts sucking on her teat and closes her eyes. I relax. I can't believe I am getting to do this. I am already in love with them all!

Chelsea, Maisy and I have sorted out who will look after each of the nine babies. We have named them already:

| Maisy | Chelsea | Juliet |
|---|---|---|
| 3 ringtail possums: Ruby, Lucy and Lambchop (he is very chubby!). | 3 healthy baby brushtail possums: Blossom, Honey and Shadow. | 2 sugar gliders: Daisy and Minnie (same pouch). A smaller brushtail called Oscar (his own pouch). |
| They like to be raised together in a little group so they are all in one big pouch. | They like to be in pouches on their own. | |

I hear a roar from outside. 'Mum!' calls Max, sticking his head in the door.

'SHHHH!' we say together.

Max tries to whisper. 'Dad's helped me set up my lizard tank and now we're looking for snails and grasshoppers for it to eat. Can I have him soon? I'm gonna call him Killer.'

'He's going to get way too attached to that lizard,' I say to Chelsea, shaking my head.

'Mmm, I know,' she says, as we look down at our babies adoringly.

'Can Chelsea and I keep our babies in my room, Mum? Max is allowed to have his lizard in his room. Maisy's mum is going to let her keep hers in her room . . . ' Maisy nods.

'Actually, I can't keep them at my house because of Princess,' says Chelsea. Princess is Chelsea's beautiful cat.

'They're not pets, Juliet.' Mum is looking really tired and frustrated as she tries to get the tiny koala to take his bottle. He keeps rolling into a ball and tucking his head down. His little back legs are bandaged and obviously very sore.

'We won't get them out unless it's feeding time, we promise,' I say. 'We just want to set it up like a little hospital where everything is quiet.'

Mum sighs. 'You're going to have to

ask Dad. You haven't got a great track record for managing to keep animals *in* your room in the past, Juliet. And I'll need to check on them every day. Mrs Brown is going to be keeping a very close eye on Maisy's possums.'

Maisy nods again vigorously.

'When they get a bit older and need to go into the cages for climbing practice and stuff, I promise we'll bring them back out here,' I plead.

Mum just looks at me. I decide I'd better leave it at that.

After we have fed all the babies, Mrs Brown takes Maisy and all of their patients home to get organised. Chelsea and I go into my room to see how it can be set up – once I've told Dad about it, of course.

'Um, maybe we should clear away a bit of this mess first?' says Chelsea.

'Good thinking,' I say as I look at the floor. Well, what I can see of it that's not hidden by clothes and books. I push it all under the bed and pull the bedspread up. I clear my desk into a box with one swipe and look around with my hands on my hips. 'There. Tidy. Now, let's go and get their cages.'

Chelsea grimaces and smiles. She *is* a bit of a neat freak.

As we walk past Max's room I can see Dad has set up the glass tank for him on his desk. There are dinosaurs surrounding it, staring in at the lizard.

'I hope they don't scare it,' I say.

'They're his friends,' Max says
confidently.

We head out to the shed to get the
first load of cages and pet carriers.
Back in my room, we place them
side by side. It really does look like a
hospital.

'I'll make labels for their cages with
their names and the times they need
to be fed and how much to feed them,'
says Chelsea, sitting down at the
computer.

'I'll go back out to the surgery to get
some teats and bottles,' I reply.

Being a vet can be very busy work.

I meet Chelsea's mum and my dad on the way. She's just been up to the pet warehouse to get some more teats for Mum and has a present for Max and his lizard; it's a box of crickets. Dad is very pleased because now he can stop hunting for bugs.

'I didn't even know they sold bugs in boxes!' says Dad, holding it up with two fingers to look inside.

'Oh, they sell all sorts of things for reptiles to eat, even boxes of cockroaches!'

Dad pulls a face. 'Thanks for not getting those, Helen! Even if the lizard prefers cockroaches, I certainly don't.'

# CHAPTER 6

## Vets Can't Get Too Attached to their Patients

I guess someone should have supervised Max putting the crickets into the tank with the lizard.

Instead of putting the cricket container into the tank and then taking the lid off, he thought he would just get one cricket out at a time and pop it in.

'Agh, get them off me!' he screeches as Chelsea and I race into his room. There are crickets leaping out of

47

the container in every direction.
Dad comes running in, but it's too
late – they've disappeared under the
bed and through his toys.

'Well, at least he got *some* in there,'
I say, trying to calm Dad down a bit.
There are about half a dozen crickets
jumping around inside the tank. The

lizard just lies there watching them.

'When's he gonna eat them?' Max presses his face against the glass.

'He might be a bit too sore to eat for a while,' Mum says from the doorway. She's come in from the surgery for the first time that day. 'Give him time to recover. I think he'll be all right.'

Dad goes to make Mum a cup of tea.

'Did you get the baby koala to drink?' I ask her.

'No.' Mum runs her hands through her hair. 'He's the only one that's not responding. I've given him a needle with some fluids, but if he doesn't pick up soon, I don't know that he'll make it. He's just too dehydrated.'

After Mum finishes her tea she goes and has a sleep. Chelsea and I offer to keep an eye on the surgery. We'll have to feed all the babies again in a couple of hours and poor Mum and Mrs O'Sullivan are going to have to get up at least twice during the night. I'm glad our babies are older and stronger.

The babies in the surgery seem warm and settled. The little koala doesn't move when I gently place my hand on the outside of the pouch. Even though he feels warm, he is shaking. I can see why Mum is so worried.

When Mum wakes up, she looks on the internet for information on orphan koalas.

'They're not like possums and gliders,' I hear her telling Dad. 'Only about ten per cent of them survive when they are brought in for care and this one has burns and shock to deal with as well.'

Mum comes to sit with us when we get ready to feed our babies for the second time. She looks pleased and says they're all doing very well.

'Chelsea and I have come to an arrangement,' I tell Mum as I sit dabbing at a tiny sugar glider's bottom. 'I clean all the bottoms and she makes up the bottles.'

Chelsea walks in with a tray of tiny labelled bottles. 'Maisy said she'd do it for me, but we didn't think about the times when she wasn't here. Poo is just not my thing. I'm sorry, Mrs Fletcher.' She looks a bit embarrassed, but Mum just smiles.

'I think that's a very clever arrangement,' she says. 'Make sure you give your hands a good wash before you feed them, Juliet.'

We all sit very quietly as each baby is fed. Their little eyes peer up at us through the dim light.

'I wonder what they're thinking?' I whisper.

'The instinct to survive is the *most* powerful thing,' says Mum. She strokes Blossom's tiny head as

Chelsea feeds her. 'They are probably very confused and frightened at the moment, but their bodies know they need this milk to survive, so that overpowers the fear.'

'Will they always be frightened of us?'

'Quite the opposite,' whispers Mum. 'After a while they'll start to see you as their mum. They'll be quite happy to climb up to your shoulder and look at the world, just like they would their real mum.'

Right on cue, Daisy, the larger of my two gliders, climbs up onto my arm as I feed her little sister.

'Hello, Daisy,' I whisper. 'I'm going to be your mummy.'

'So are they ever going to want to leave us?' asks Chelsea. The thought of going everywhere with three possums clinging to her is obviously not the most exciting news for her. I wouldn't mind at all.

'That's why they'll go to a release aviary out in the bush when they don't need a bottle any more. A carer will put food and water out for them until they are adjusted to the foods and surroundings of their natural environment and humans gradually have less and less contact with them. Then they are released back into the wild.'

'I must make a note of all the stages they have to go through later,' I say to myself. Handing them over to the carer was going to be a very sad day.

# CHAPTER 7

## Vets Like the Sound of the Bush

We all get into bed feeling exhausted. It's been another long, tiring day. As well as caring for the new babies, I still have my guinea pigs, chickens and Curly to look after. I feel really guilty as I put Curly's basket outside my bedroom door. I don't think he likes my new babies at all.

Only a couple of minutes after Dad turns off the light in the hallway, the crickets start to chirp.

'Oh, for goodness sakes!' groans Dad.

I don't mind the noise at all. It's a
bit like sleeping out in the bush. In
fact, I think my babies actually like it
because they settle. It probably makes
them feel more like they're at home.

I get up to go to the toilet during
the night and see the light on in the
surgery.

I tiptoe out along the path and open
the door. Mum looks up and doesn't
seem all that surprised to see me. Mrs
O'Sullivan is sitting beside her feeding
a baby too.

'How's the baby koala?' I ask.

'Still struggling, I'm afraid,' sighs
Mum. 'I did get her to take a tiny
sip of milk from a glass syringe, but

she's very reluctant.'

I walk over and look into her cage. The little ball inside the pouch doesn't move at all.

'Juliet, vets can't save every animal that comes in. You know that.'

I nod and try to smile. 'I think I'll go back to bed.'

Curly has followed me the whole time. I let him into my room to see what he will do. He sniffs at the cages for a moment then sits beside the bed and rests his chin on it. I stroke him gently. He seems to understand that I feel sad.

❖

The next morning Max is very excited.

His lizard has eaten some of the banana from his bowl.

'That's a good sign,' says Mum.

'It'll be a better sign when he's eaten those crickets,' grumbles Dad, looking behind the door and in the wardrobe. I don't think Dad would make much of a camper.

'My dinosaurs are going to help me round up the crickets,' says Max proudly. I look at a large Tyrannosaurus Rex on the floor with its mouth open. A cricket is sitting on its nose. I don't think it's quite as terrified as Max might hope.

'Just make sure it's a quiet hunt,' I say. 'My babies are trying to sleep.'

Chelsea arrives from next door looking all neat and tidy. I look like a dinosaur's breakfast. Vets don't always have time for grooming themselves.

We start getting ready for our next round of feeding, preparing the warm water and formula.

'Maisy and her mum are bringing their babies in for a check-up with your mum this morning,' says Chelsea.

'I can't wait to see those little ringtail possums again. Especially Lambchop. He's so chubby and cuddly looking.'

'I don't understand why they're called ringtails?' says Chelsea. 'My brushtails all have tails that make little rings too.' She pulls back one of the pouches to reveal a fluffy tail curled in the shape of a ring.

'Yeah, it's confusing,' I say. 'All possums have tails that go into a ring because that's how they hold onto branches and stuff. Brushtail possums just have much fluffier ones – a bit like a bottlebrush, I guess. Here, I'll show you the difference.'

I open my Vet Diary.

### Common Brushtail
- Larger than ringtails – can get to be the size of a large cat
- Black bushy tail (usually no white tip)
- Longish grey fur

### Common Ringtail
- Smaller than brushtails
- Shorter fur
- Usually a dark reddish colour
- Short fur on tail with white tip at the end

Common Brushtail

Common Ringtail

'Oh, I see! Juliet,' sighs Chelsea, 'you really *are* nearly a vet.'

I smile but the moment is ruined by a loud 'Gotcha!' Max runs past the bedroom yelling, 'Dad, I got another one!'

'I don't know how much longer this can go on,' I mutter as I stand up to close my door. 'This morning Curly was fast asleep when a cricket crawled onto his back. Max pounced on it and poor Curly got such a fright he ran out the back door taking the screen with him. Dad's just finished fixing it now.'

'That's not going to do a lot for your Dad's love of animals!' laughs Chelsea.

Right on cue we hear a loud 'AGGGHHHH!' followed by a bang in the kitchen. We both race out to see what it is.

'What on earth?' yells Dad. An ice-cream tub half-filled with writhing brown things is sitting on the table.

'Mealworms,' Max and I answer in unison.

'What are mealworms?' says Dad, pulling a face. 'And why do we have worms of any kind in the fridge? I thought it was leftovers from dinner last night.'

'They're to feed Killer the Lizard,' Max explains. 'Mrs O'Sullivan bought them for me because we were worried the crickets were too fast for the lizard while he's sick. You should see how much he loves them, Dad.'

'They're not actually worms, Dad. They're beetle larvae. If you keep them in the fridge, it stops them from going through metamorphosis,' I add.

I thought everyone knew that.

'Here, I'm sure I have a life-cycle

diagram in my Vet Diary.'

I flick through to the section on insects to find my diagram.

'Uh, thanks, Juliet, but I think . . . I'm just going to . . . um . . . work in my . . . office . . . alone . . . for a while,' says Dad, backing away slowly before I can show him. He leaves the kitchen shaking his head. He's been doing that a lot lately.

# CHAPTER
# 8

## Vets Love Seeing Healthy Animals

Maisy and her mum arrive and bring
Harry, Maisy's little brother, with
them. He has a cardboard box full of
dinosaurs in his arms. Just what we
need. More dinosaurs. They can't wait
to show us all their healthy babies.

'Look at the size of them now!'
laughs Mum as Maisy holds up
Lambchop, Lucy and Ruby. Their little
bulging black eyes peer curiously at
all of us as they hang onto Maisy's
fingers. She snuggles them into her

chest. 'Lambchop weighs 250 grams already,' she announces proudly.

'Thank you all for doing this,' Mum says as she peeps into a pouch at a tiny brushtail possum, 'I don't know what I would've done without you all.'

'Actually, Helen and I have decided to become registered wildlife carers,' Chelsea's mum announces. 'We feel like this is such a worthwhile thing to do and with so many animals dying in the fire, we have to all work together to rebuild the populations.'

'Does that mean we can become carers too?' Chelsea says excitedly.

'Not until you and Maisy are older,' says Mum, 'but if both your mums are carers, they'll always need help. And you have proved yourselves to be very capable in this emergency.'

We all go over to Chelsea's house to see how her mum is going. She is still sewing little pouches to send to the other carers in the area.

'Muuuuuuuummmmmm!' there is a loud cry from Max in the backyard. We all rush out to see.

'We were just taking Killer out for a walk on the grass with our other dinosaurs and he took off and went under the woodpile. Can you catch him, Mum? Can you get him back?'

'I think Killer might be trying to tell you something, Max. I think he is ready to be free.'

'But he hasn't eaten all his crickets yet,' he wails, 'or his mealworms!'

Mum bobs down and pulls Max close. I start to worry that I am going to cry too. Max loves Killer like I love my babies. 'You know what would be really nice, Max? If you got some crickets and mealworms and put them with a bowl of water out here near the woodpile for Killer. Then he won't have to go too far away to hunt for his food.'

'We can put some snails under there for him too,' Harry adds.

Max brightens. 'He'd love that,' he sniffles as they head inside to get the mealworms. 'I just really liked having him in my room.'

Chelsea, Maisy and I walk over to the surgery to look in on the animals Mum is caring for. We stand at the cage quietly and watch the tiny koala. He keeps struggling and trying to push his way out of the pouch.

'He's taking a little more milk, but it's such a struggle. He's so unsettled and he's losing weight,' sighs Mum.

'He looks like he's looking for his mum,' says Chelsea sadly.

'Chelsea, you are brilliant!' I whisper. 'You really do have a talent with animal behaviour and you have just given me a great idea.'

I race back inside and start pulling

stuff out from under my bed.

'Didn't you just shove all that under there?' says Chelsea, confused.

'Yep,' I say, trying to find what I'm hunting for. Then my hand touches something. 'Got it!'

I pull out a large brown teddy. 'One koala mummy,' I smile.

We race outside and carefully open the door to the cage. All we can see is the top of the little koala's head. I gently put the pouch against the teddy's tummy and we all wait.

A tiny hand comes out and curls around the teddy's fur. Ever so slowly the little koala emerges from the pouch and nestles in under the tummy of the large bear. Their furs seem to blend together and all we can see is his little black button nose poking out from under the bear's arm. We all look at each other and smile.

'I think your name should be Button,' I whisper.

# CHAPTER 9

## Being a Vet Can Be Time-Consuming

'Our babies have really grown, haven't they?' I say excitedly.

Chelsea, Maisy and I are weighing them all and filling in their charts.

'Mum says all the brushtail possums that are over 200 grams and the ringtails that are over 130 grams can start being fed some strained fruit and custards now. Soon they will start to nibble at leaves and flowers.'

'Well, that is all three of my babies,'

says Chelsea. 'They look so much better than they did three weeks ago, don't they!'

'And mine,' smiles Maisy, holding up an adorable and very chubby little Lambchop. 'At least your mum won't have to give them bottles during the day when we are at school now. We can just do an early morning, afternoon and night feed.'

'Let's go and see what Mum wants us to start with,' I say. 'My Oscar's still a bit small but the sugar gliders are coming along well. I wonder if they'll start on solids soon too?'

Mum is in the surgery feeding Button, the baby koala. We call him

Button because he has a little button
nose that he always pokes out of
his pouch first when he comes out
for feeding. He is sitting up high on
his teddy mother's back, slurping
vigorously at his bottle. He turns his
head to look at us but doesn't take the
teat out of his mouth.

'He's such a guts,' laughs Mum.
She gives him a little pat on his fluffy
bottom. 'The teddy bear was such a
good idea, girls.'

We all beam proudly at each other.

'Will he ever be able to be released
into the wild again?' Maisy asks.

'I don't think so,' sighs Mum. 'His
claws and pads on his back feet are

very badly scarred, so he is probably better off in a sanctuary where he won't have to climb fast to escape predators.'

For a moment we look sadly at Button, but then he buries his head into the teddy's soft fur.

'At least he'll get to keep his teddy!' laughs Chelsea. 'He looks pretty attached to it.'

'What should we start to feed our possums on now, Mum?' I ask. 'Six of them have reached their goal weight for solid food.'

'Start with a little bit of stewed apples and banana custard. I bought some little cans and put them in the pantry. Just offer them a little on a spoon first, then we can start to leave a bowl out for them to help themselves.'

'Mum thinks maybe mine are ready for a cage now, Mrs Fletcher,' says Maisy.

'They are, Maisy. There are plenty in the surgery you can choose from. As they grow they will need bigger cages with branches to climb on and lots of leaves and flowers to choose from. You can help decorate their cages. By the time they reach 800 grams, they won't need milk at all and they can go to release aviaries.'

'How do they work?' asks Chelsea.

'They are large cages in the area where the animal will eventually roam free. Once it has had time to get used to the surroundings, the door or roof is opened so that it can start to become a wild animal again,' explains Mum.

'Where will we release ours?' I ask quietly, trying not to look worried.

'A carer that lives in the mountains where the possums came from told me she has some outdoor release aviaries we can use.'

Mum looks at me. She knows how I am feeling.

'I guess they need to be free,' says Chelsea.

I desperately want to change the subject. 'Should my gliders be having solid food yet?' I ask. 'They weigh about 30 grams each.'

'You'll know when they are ready. At about 35 grams they will start to explore their surrounds and look for ways to escape. You can offer them a few little things and see how they like them. They are a bit different to possums, because they are mainly insectivores – that means they eat insects – so they need a lot more protein.'

I whip out my Vet Diary and take some notes as Mum tells us what they eat.

- custard
- yoghurt
- baby cereal
- fruit
- eggs
- shelled sunflower seeds
- cat and dog food pellets
- rice
- pasta
- veggies
- a little bit of cooked mince
- insectivore mix
- bark
- flowers

We spend the rest of the afternoon setting up cages for Chelsea to put her possums in. We make sure they have a warm, dark box with bedding, branches, water and food. Chelsea has a real talent for cage decorating. Maybe she could become a world famous animal trainer *and* pet cage decorator.

Maisy's mum has some old chook

cages at home that Maisy can use to do the same thing for her babies.

That night I am lying in my bed and can hear my little gliders and Oscar moving around in their pouches and pet carriers. At first I didn't sleep much when I could hear them moving around, but now I don't know how I'll sleep when they're gone. They really are starting to become nocturnal and wanting to come out at night. Mum's right. It won't be long before my babies need to go out into the surgery cages too. I feel really sad and wonder if mother possums feel sad when their babies leave their pouches for the last time. Or birds whose babies leave their nests? I get my gliders out for a cuddle, even though they don't need feeding. Being a vet can make your heart ache. I am so glad I don't have to let Curly and my other pets go. I just wish I could keep them *all*.

# CHAPTER 10

## Vets Have to Say Goodbye a Lot

More than a month later, Mum and I are cleaning out the cages in her surgery when the door suddenly flies open and Max yells, 'He's back!'

'Who's back?' calls Mum, as the door slams shut and Max disappears.

The door swings open again and Max's face pokes around it. 'Killer, of course!'

We race outside to see the sandpit full of dinosaurs, as usual. Dad has been called too, but he stands at a safe distance with his coffee.

'Look,' points Max, 'in the middle. He's come back to visit his friends. I told you he liked them, Juliet. I told you they were his friends.'

I shake my head and smile at the large blue-tongue lizard soaking up the sun in the sandpit in the middle of all Max's plastic dinosaurs.

'See, Juliet,' boasts Max. 'I *could* be a vet too.'

Dad nearly chokes on his coffee.

'Well, you vets better get dressed and ready because we are due at the Brown's dairy in one hour.' Mum smiles and scruffs Max's hair. I'd like to scruff Max's neck.

We all drive out to the dairy later that afternoon. Even Dad comes. Tonight it's time for Maisy's possums to be set free because they have reached their goal weight.

Mrs Brown has converted her old chook pens in the orchard into release aviaries for Maisy's possums. Chelsea, Maisy and I helped set them up with lovely trees to climb in and boxes to hide in. Whenever Mum visits the dairy, Chelsea and I go along and whisper to them through the wire. I'm sure they remember us as they peer out from their little homes.

All of our families sit quietly on rugs in the paddock with a picnic dinner as the sun sets and the night sky settles over us. It is a calm, still night with lots of stars and the crickets chirping around us make me smile. I glance over at Dad. He's sitting on the esky, carefully checking the rug under his feet for creepy crawlies.

When it's time, Mr Brown takes his ladder and slowly pulls back a door in the roof of the release aviary.

There is a thick rope that leads from the hole to the high branches of the nearest tree, the apple tree.

While we wait, I look at the sketch of the release aviary that I did in my Vet Diary.

Release Aviary

'I can't see them,' says Max.

'Be patient,' Mum says in a low voice, 'they'll take a while to feel brave enough to come out.'

'I see Lambchop!' whispers Maisy excitedly. 'Look, he's the size of a rockmelon!'

We all chuckle quietly.

'I hope they find the rope,' says Mrs O'Sullivan, as two more plump brown balls appear from their boxes and crawl up to sit near Lambchop on a branch.

We wait for at least ten minutes and Max and Harry start to poke each other and wrestle on the rug. Dad is asking Mr Brown whether snakes are nocturnal.

At last Lambchop sees the rope and starts the long climb up it and through the hole into the apple tree, his little hands clinging easily to the rope. The other fat, brown possums shuffle after him.

Everyone gives a small cheer and Chelsea smiles at me a bit sadly.

I look over at Maisy and see that she seems genuinely happy.

'I guess they're not meant to be pets in little cages,' I say quietly.

'No,' Chelsea laughs as Lambchop leans over to pluck a juicy flower from its stem and stuffs it into his mouth. 'I guess they're not.'

'Goodbye, babies,' I whisper to myself as I think about how sad it will be to let my little gliders go. Sometimes doing the right thing is the hardest thing of all, and vets have to learn that.

# Quiz! Are You Nearly a Vet?

1. **What do you call a baby possum?**
   a. A kitten
   b. A cub
   c. A joey
   d. A puggle

2. **What did Juliet find under her bed for the baby koala?**
   a. Her lunch from three weeks ago
   b. A teddy bear
   c. One of Max's dinosaurs
   d. Three sheep

3. **Before you feed a baby possum you should:**
   a. Give it a big cuddle and a kiss
   b. Put on its bib so it doesn't dribble
   c. Sing it a nursery rhyme
   d. Wipe its bottom to make it go to the toilet

4. **Blue-tongue lizards love to eat:**
   a. Snails
   b. Ice-cream
   c. Small children
   d. Fish and chips

5. **Why did the girls have to let their babies go?**
   a. They were wild animals and should not be kept as pets
   b. They would get sick of looking after them
   c. The possums would be scared of Max's dinosaurs
   d. All the kids at school would want one

6. It was strange to see Juliet's dad holding a possum because:
a. He prefers snakes
b. Animals don't usually like him
c. He doesn't usually like animals
d. He's not very strong

7. What did Juliet's mum put on the wombat's feet?
a. Slippers
b. Ice packs
c. Ice skates
d. Vegemite

8. What escaped in Max's room?
a. Dinosaurs
b. Cockroaches
c. Crickets
d. A sugar glider

9. What does Max like to have for breakfast on Saturdays?
a. Cereal
b. Pancakes
c. Bacon and eggs
d. Porridge

10. All baby mammals drink:
a. Juice
b. Soft drink
c. Cordial
d. Milk

**Answers** : 1c, 2b, 3d, 4a, 5a, 6c, 7b, 8c, 9b, 10d. Well done!

## From Rebecca Johnson

My dad was never the kind of man who was all that 'into' pets, but I have seen him stop his car to usher a snake from the road and go to an enormous amount of trouble to unhook fish to release them. My mum loves all things with a beating heart, and will go out of her way to rescue (and feed) any creature she sees needing help – regardless of its size or number of legs. Both my parents taught me compassion for all animals.

## From Kyla May

As a little girl, I always wanted to be a vet. I had mice, guinea pigs, dogs, goldfish, sea snails, sea monkeys and tadpoles as pets. I loved looking after my friends' pets when they went on holidays and every Saturday I helped out at a pet store. Now that I'm all grown up, I have the best job in the world. I get to draw lots of animals for children's books and for animated TV shows. In my studio I have two dogs, Jed and Evie, and two cats, Bosco and Kobe, who love to watch me draw.

Look out for the new **Juliet** nearly a **Vet** books:

- Beach Buddies
- Zookeeper for a Day
- The Lost Dogs
- Playground Pets